For my family
—SC

For Jim and Raechele
—JT

tiger tales
an imprint of ME Media, LLC
202 Old Ridgefield Road, Wilton, CT 06897
Published in the United States 2003
Originally published in Great Britain 2000
By Little Tiger Press
An imprint of Magi Publications
Text copyright ©2000 Sheridan Cain
Illustrations copyright ©2000 Jack Tickle
CIP data is available
ISBN 1-58925-025-7
Printed in Belgium
1 3 5 7 9 10 8 6 4 2

The Crunching Munching Caterpillar

by Sheridan Cain

Illustrated by
Jack Tickle

tiger tales

Caterpillar was always hungry. For weeks he crunched and munched his way through the fresh, juicy leaves of a blackberry bush.

Bzzzzzzzz

One day, Caterpillar was about to crunch into another leaf when...

Crunch
Crunch

Munch
Munch

Bzzzzzzzzzzzzz

Bumblebee landed
beside him!

"Wow!" said Caterpillar.
"How did you get here?"
"Simple," said Bumblebee.
"I have wings. Look!"
"Oh, I'd like some of
those," said Caterpillar.

Bumblebee flew up into the air and buzzed busily from flower to flower.

Bzzzzz

Bzzzz

"I'd love to fly like that," said Caterpillar.

"Well, you can't," said Bumblebee. "I've got wings, and you've got legs. Your legs are for walking."

"I guess so," sighed Caterpillar.

Bzzzzoommm

Bumblebee flew off to the next bush. Watching
Bumblebee fly had made Caterpillar *very* hungry,
so he crunched and he munched
until it was time for bed.

Crunch Munch
Crunch Munch
Yaw-w-n!

Caterpillar woke to the sound of twittering. Birds swooped and soared in the early morning light.

Caterpillar was just about to start his breakfast when...

Sparrow landed
beside him.

"I'd love to fly high in the air like that," said Caterpillar.

"Well, you can't," said Sparrow. "You need to be as light as the dandelion fluff that floats on the breeze. You're far too big to fly. Your legs are for walking."

"I guess so," said Caterpillar sadly.

Caterpillar kept on crunching and munching all day and into the evening, when the sun began to set.

Crunch
Munch

Crunch
Munch

He wrapped a leaf around himself to keep
warm. He was just about to go to sleep when...

Butterfly landed gracefully beside him.

"Oh, I wish I could fly like you," sighed Caterpillar. "But I'm too big and I have legs instead of wings."

Butterfly smiled a secret, knowing smile. "Who knows? Perhaps one day you will fly, light as a feather, like me," she said. "But now, little Caterpillar, you should go to sleep. You look very tired."

Butterfly was right. Caterpillar suddenly felt very sleepy.

As Butterfly flew off into the night sky, he fell into a deep, deep sleep.

Caterpillar slept all through the winter,
and his sleep was filled with dreams.

He dreamed he had wings and was soaring in the blue sky above the tall trees...

He dreamed he was a piece of dandelion fluff, drifting toward the sun.

He dreamed he was as light as a feather, floating on the breeze.

When Caterpillar woke up he felt the warmth of the spring sun. He was stiff from his long sleep, but he did not feel very hungry. He stretched and stretched . . .

and a breeze lifted
Caterpillar into the air.

Caterpillar was no longer
short and plump. He had
WINGS! Great, big, wonderful
BUTTERFLY WINGS!

"Wow!" he said. "I'm flying! I'm really flying!"